ARTIFICIAL INTELLIGENCE: HOW IT CHANGED THE WORLD

TECHNOLOGY IS THE THING WE NEEDED , BUT WE REALLY NEED IT THAT ??

SAM RAMSEY

Made with ♥ on the Notion Press Platform
www.notionpress.com

FOR THE HUMANS

Contents

Contents

Preface

This book not in against any kind of thing's which is happening currently in a world right now, but yeah we keep hoping everything will be fine in future, like no war , no disease, no virus, no hard technology who make people weak day by day, in a hope god will protect us.

.

sometimes harsh truth is bit more difficult to swallow.

- S.M

Prologue

Remember the Year or time when did the last time you spend some quality time with your friends & family or loved ones, in real world not just only in a social media, see you don't have a answer it's that right HELL yeah; This is not just only about the Technologies or distance we're making right now' for ourselves.

.

We all watched movies like war of the worlds, Or read one the best sci-fi novel by H.G wells ; The time machine.we all know what will happened if we depend on advance technologies like AI-artificial intelligence what's the result after if we do keep using it, so why we kept supporting technologies and making our world difficult for ours children and their's Future. There are both Pros or Cons so Be aware what we are Doing .

CHAPTER I

Intro-Define

Artificial Intelligence, commonly known as AI, is a rapidly-evolving field in computer science that focuses on creating computer systems and algorithms that can perform tasks that would normally require human intelligence. The goal of AI is to create systems that can learn from data, identify patterns, and make predictions or decisions based on that learning, just as a human being would. AI is designed to help machines and systems think and reason in a way that resembles human thought processes.

There are two main categories of AI: narrow AI and general AI. Narrow AI focuses on developing systems that can perform specific tasks, such as speech recognition, image classification, and decision-making. These systems are designed to be highly specialized and perform one task very well. On the other hand, general AI aims to create systems that can perform any intellectual task that a human being can, such as problem-solving, decision-making, and understanding natural language.

AI is an interdisciplinary field that draws on computer science, mathematics, psychology, engineering, and many other fields to create intelligent machines and systems. AI systems are typically trained on large datasets, which allow them to learn from patterns in the data and make predictions or decisions based on that learning. AI systems can also be trained through reinforcement learning, which involves learning from experience and adjusting their behavior based on the outcomes of their actions.

In recent years, AI has made significant progress, driven by the development of technologies such as machine learning, deep learning, and natural language processing. These advances have enabled the creation of more advanced AI systems that can perform a wider range of tasks and make more sophisticated predictions and decisions. AI has already transformed many industries, including healthcare, finance, retail, and transportation, and it is expected to play an even larger role in our lives in the future.

However, as with any new technology, AI also raises important ethical and societal questions that must be addressed. For example, as AI systems become more sophisticated, there are concerns about their ability to make decisions that could have significant impacts on people's lives, such as in the areas of healthcare or criminal justice. Additionally, there are questions about the potential impact of AI on the job market, as some jobs may become automated and others may change.

Artificial Intelligence is a rapidly-evolving field that has the potential to transform our lives in many positive ways, but it also raises important ethical and societal questions that must be addressed as the technology continues to develop

History of developmennt

The history of Artificial Intelligence (AI) is a long and fascinating one, dating back to the mid-20th century when computer scientists first began to explore the idea of creating machines that could perform tasks that normally require human intelligence. The development of AI as a field of study can be traced back to a seminal conference that was held in 1956 at Dartmouth College in Hanover, New Hampshire. This conference marked the beginning of the modern era of AI research, and it brought together computer scientists, engineers, and researchers who were interested in exploring the potential of machines to perform tasks that were previously thought to be the exclusive domain of humans.

In the early days of AI, the focus was on developing systems that could perform specific tasks, such as playing chess or solving mathematical problems. This led to the development of expert systems, which were designed to solve specific problems by drawing on knowledge from a specific domain. However, the early systems were limited in their capabilities, and they were only able to perform tasks that were well defined and structured.

In the 1980s and 1990s, AI made significant progress due to advances in computer hardware and software, which enabled the creation of more sophisticated AI systems. This period saw the development of machine learning, a branch of AI that focused on creating algorithms that could learn from data, identify patterns, and make predictions based on that learning. Additionally, the development of expert systems gave way to more advanced systems, such as knowledge-based systems and rule-based systems, which were able to perform a wider range of tasks.

The 21st century has been a period of rapid growth for AI, driven by the development of technologies such as deep learning and natural language processing. These advances have enabled the creation of more advanced AI systems that can perform a wider range of tasks and make more sophisticated predictions and decisions. The widespread availability of large datasets has also played a key role in the development of AI, as these datasets have enabled AI systems to learn from patterns in the data and make more accurate predictions and decisions.

Today, AI is having a major impact on many industries, including healthcare, finance, retail, and transportation, and it is expected to play an even larger role in our lives in the future. The field of AI is continuing to evolve and advance, with researchers and developers exploring new ways to create more advanced AI systems and tackle some of the major challenges facing the field. These challenges include ensuring the ethical and responsible use of AI, improving the transparency and explainability of AI systems, and developing systems that are more robust and secure.

The history of AI is a story of rapid progress and growth, driven by advances in technology, computer science, and

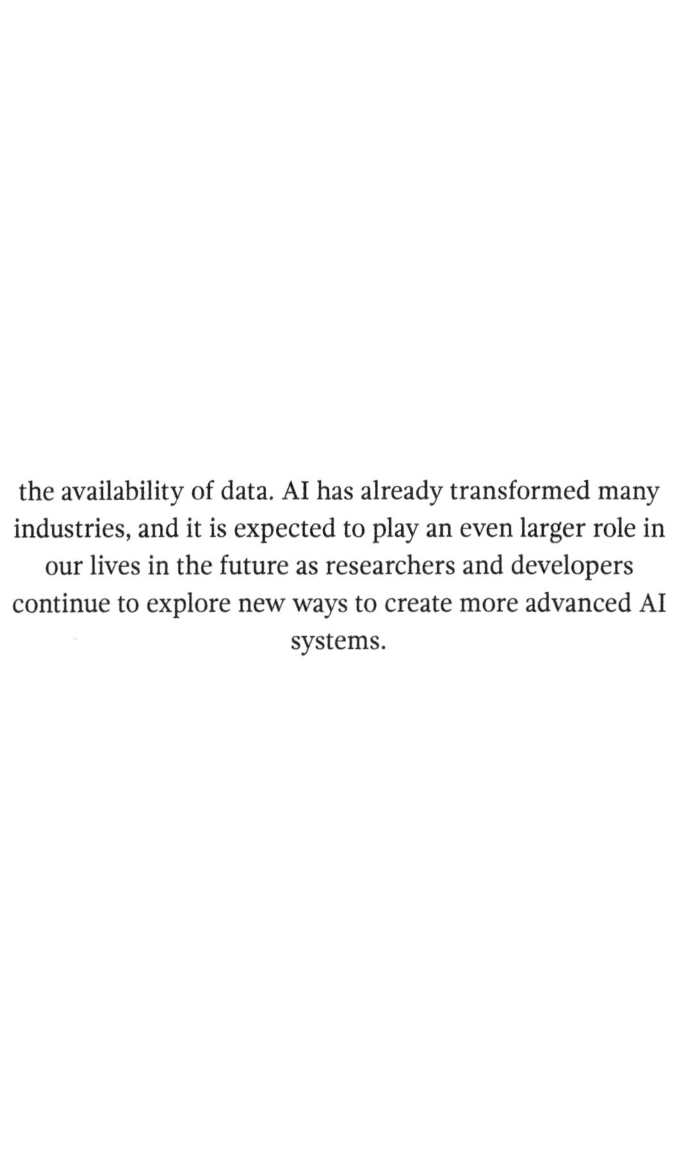

the availability of data. AI has already transformed many industries, and it is expected to play an even larger role in our lives in the future as researchers and developers continue to explore new ways to create more advanced AI systems.

Overview of the impact of AI on the world

Artificial Intelligence (AI) has had a profound impact on the world, transforming many industries and changing the way we live and work. AI is a branch of computer science that deals with the creation of intelligent machines that can perform tasks that normally require human intelligence, such as recognizing patterns, making predictions, and solving problems.

One of the biggest impacts of AI has been in the field of automation, where AI systems are being used to automate many routine tasks, such as data entry and analysis. This has led to increased efficiency and productivity in many industries, as well as freeing up human workers to focus on more complex and creative tasks.

AI has also had a significant impact on the healthcare industry, where it is being used to improve diagnosis and treatment, as well as to develop new medicines and therapies. For example, AI systems are being used to analyze large amounts of medical data to identify new treatments for diseases, and to develop personalized medicine plans for patients based on their individual genetic profiles.

In the financial industry, AI is being used to improve risk management, detect fraud, and make more informed investment decisions. AI systems are able to analyze large amounts of financial data to identify patterns and make predictions, which can help banks and other financial institutions make more informed decisions and reduce their exposure to risk.

AI is also having a major impact on the retail industry, where it is being used to personalize shopping experiences, improve supply chain management, and increase efficiency in the distribution of goods. For example, AI systems are being used to analyze customer data and make recommendations on products, and to optimize inventory management and distribution networks.

The impact of AI on the world has been far-reaching and profound, transforming many industries and changing the way we live and work. While there are still many challenges to overcome, such as ensuring the ethical and responsible use of AI, the future of AI looks very promising, and it is expected to continue to have a major impact on the world in the years to come.

CHAPTER II

AI in Business and Industry

Artificial Intelligence (AI) has had a significant impact on the business and industry sectors, transforming the way companies operate and compete in today's marketplace. AI is being used in many different ways to increase efficiency, reduce costs, improve customer experiences, and gain a competitive edge.

One of the key areas where AI is having an impact is automation, where AI systems are being used to automate many routine tasks, such as data entry, customer service, and supply chain management. Automation not only increases efficiency and reduces costs, but it also frees up human workers to focus on more complex and creative tasks.

In the customer service sector, AI is being used to enhance customer experiences by providing personalized support, responding to customer inquiries, and solving problems. AI systems, such as chatbots and virtual assistants, are able to handle large volumes of customer interactions, and provide quick and accurate responses, helping companies to improve customer satisfaction and loyalty.

In the marketing sector, AI is being used to analyze large amounts of customer data to better understand consumer behavior, and to develop targeted marketing campaigns. AI systems are able to analyze customer data, such as purchase history and social media activity, to identify patterns and make predictions, helping companies to better understand their customers and reach them more effectively.

In the supply chain and logistics sector, AI is being used to optimize production and distribution networks, reduce waste, and improve delivery times. AI systems are able to analyze vast amounts of data to identify bottlenecks, and to optimize production and delivery routes, helping companies to improve efficiency and reduce costs.

In the financial sector, AI is being used to improve risk management, detect fraud, and make more informed investment decisions. AI systems are able to analyze large amounts of financial data to identify patterns and make predictions, which can help banks and other financial institutions make more informed decisions and reduce their exposure to risk.

AI is having a significant impact on the business and industry sectors, transforming the way companies operate and compete in today's marketplace. As AI technology continues to advance, it is expected to have an even greater impact in the future, helping companies to become more efficient, innovative, and competitive.

Automation and job displacement

Automation, driven by the advancement of Artificial Intelligence (AI) technology, has the potential to displace some jobs and alter the nature of work in many industries. As AI systems become more capable of performing routine and repetitive tasks, there is a risk that some jobs may become redundant, leading to job losses and unemployment.

However, it is important to note that automation has also led to the creation of new jobs in areas such as software development, data analysis, and AI engineering. While some jobs may become obsolete, new job opportunities are also emerging as a result of automation.

Additionally, automation can lead to increased efficiency and productivity in many industries, which can ultimately benefit workers by freeing up time and resources for more valuable tasks, and by enabling companies to invest in growth and innovation.

There is a need for policies and initiatives that support workers who may be impacted by automation, such as retraining programs and education initiatives to help them acquire new skills and transition to new roles. Additionally, it is important for companies to implement strategies that ensure that the benefits of automation are shared by workers, such as investing in their training and development, and promoting career mobility.

While automation and AI may result in some job displacement, it also has the potential to create new job opportunities and increase efficiency and productivity in many industries. It is important for governments and businesses to work together to manage the impact of automation and to ensure that workers are supported in adapting to the changing nature of work.

Advancements in manufacturing and supply chain

Artificial Intelligence has been making waves in the manufacturing and supply chain management industries, transforming the way these industries operate and leading to significant advancements. AI has become an invaluable tool for businesses that are looking to improve efficiency, reduce costs, and enhance the customer experience.

In the manufacturing industry, AI has been instrumental in automating many tasks that were previously done by humans. For instance, AI systems can handle tasks such as material handling and assembly, freeing up human workers to focus on more complex and creative tasks. This automation not only improves efficiency, but it also enhances safety by reducing the risk of injury to workers.

Moreover, AI is being leveraged in the manufacturing industry to optimize production processes and improve product quality. AI algorithms can analyze vast amounts of production data to identify areas where improvements can be made, such as reducing waste, streamlining processes, and enhancing product quality. By doing so, businesses can make more informed decisions and improve their overall competitiveness.

In the supply chain management industry, AI has made it possible to optimize logistics and distribution networks. By analyzing vast amounts of data, AI systems can identify the most efficient delivery routes, reducing delivery times and costs. Additionally, AI can be used to monitor deliveries in real-time, providing businesses with greater visibility and control over their supply chain operations.

AI is also being used in predictive maintenance to reduce downtime and increase equipment efficiency. AI algorithms can analyze equipment data to identify potential problems before they occur, allowing companies to perform maintenance when it is needed, rather than waiting for a breakdown. By doing so, businesses can improve equipment efficiency, reduce downtime, and ultimately improve the customer experience.

AI has had a profound impact on the manufacturing and supply chain management industries, leading to significant advancements in automation, optimization, and data analysis. By leveraging AI, businesses can become more efficient, innovative, and competitive, ultimately delivering better outcomes for their customers.

AI and big data analysis in finance and marketing

The integration of Artificial Intelligence (AI) and big data analysis has dramatically changed the way businesses operate in the finance and marketing industries. These technologies have provided companies with the tools to make informed decisions, enhance customer experiences, and improve their overall efficiency and competitiveness.

In finance, AI algorithms can process and analyze large amounts of financial data to identify patterns, anomalies, and fraudulent activity. This has improved the speed and accuracy of fraud detection and has enhanced the overall risk management of financial institutions. AI also plays a crucial role in improving customer service, by providing customers with personalized recommendations and investment advice.

In marketing, AI and big data analysis are being leveraged to personalize customer experiences and improve customer engagement. By analyzing customer data, businesses can understand their preferences, behavior, and needs, enabling them to tailor their marketing efforts and drive customer loyalty. AI is also being utilized to optimize pricing strategies, analyze customer feedback and sentiment, and improve customer retention.

In addition to personalizing customer experiences, AI and big data analysis are also being used to optimize marketing efforts and improve ROI. By analyzing customer data and feedback, businesses can identify the most effective marketing channels, improve campaign targeting, and increase the effectiveness of their marketing spend.

Big data analysis has also made it possible for businesses to gain a deeper understanding of their target markets and make data-driven decisions. By analyzing large amounts of customer data, businesses can identify market trends, customer preferences, and behavior patterns, enabling them to make more informed decisions and enhance their marketing efforts.

AI and big data analysis are having a profound impact on the finance and marketing industries, providing businesses with the tools they need to improve customer experiences, increase efficiency, and drive growth.

CHAPTER III

AI in Healthcare

Artificial Intelligence (AI) has been a game-changer in the healthcare industry, revolutionizing the way medical professionals diagnose, treat and monitor patients. AI has the potential to transform the healthcare industry and make healthcare more efficient, personalized and effective.

One of the areas where AI has made a significant impact is in diagnosis and treatment. AI algorithms can process and analyze large amounts of medical data to identify patterns and anomalies, which can lead to more accurate diagnoses and improved patient outcomes. By analyzing imaging scans, such as X-rays and MRIs, AI can assist medical professionals in identifying potential health issues, provide recommendations for further testing or treatment and even make diagnoses on its own. Furthermore, AI is being used to develop predictive models that can forecast the likelihood of diseases, allowing medical professionals to take preventative measures.

Another area where AI is making a big impact is in drug discovery and development. AI algorithms can analyze vast amounts of genetic and molecular data to identify new targets for drug development and improve the efficiency of the drug discovery process. By leveraging AI, the time and cost of bringing new treatments to market are reduced, leading to better patient outcomes.

Telemedicine is another area where AI is making a difference. AI algorithms can assist medical professionals in triaging patients, provide remote patient monitoring, and support telemedicine consultations. By leveraging AI, healthcare providers can improve patient access to care, increase the efficiency of the healthcare system, and reduce the cost of delivering care. This means that patients, especially those living in rural or remote areas, can have access to healthcare services that they may not have had access to previously.

AI has the potential to transform the healthcare industry and make healthcare more efficient, personalized, and effective. With the continued advancement of AI, the healthcare industry is poised for further transformation, leading to a future of more personalized and effective healthcare for patients. AI has the power to change the lives of people all around the world, and its impact on the healthcare industry is just one example of its far-reaching potential.

Improving medical diagnosis and treatment

Artificial Intelligence is revolutionizing the way medical diagnoses and treatments are performed, improving accuracy, speed and efficiency. AI algorithms can analyze vast amounts of data, identify patterns, and assist medical professionals in making diagnoses and developing treatments. With AI, medical professionals are able to focus on other aspects of patient care, leading to better outcomes and a more effective healthcare system. As AI technology continues to advance, the impact it will have on the healthcare industry will only continue to grow.

Personalized medicine and genomics

The application of Artificial Intelligence in the realm of personalized medicine and genomics is leading to a revolution in the healthcare industry. With AI, medical professionals are able to analyze vast amounts of genetic and molecular data to provide individuals with more targeted, personalized treatments. By leveraging AI, professionals gain a deeper understanding of the genetic basis of diseases and are able to develop more effective treatments. This integration of AI with personalized medicine and genomics is improving patient outcomes and transforming the way healthcare is delivered.

AI in drug development and clinical trials

The use of Artificial Intelligence (AI) in the field of drug development and clinical trials has caused a major shift in the way we create and test new treatments. With AI, the process is much more streamlined, efficient and effective.

In the discovery phase, AI algorithms are utilized to analyze large amounts of data and information, which leads to the identification of new drug targets and the optimization of drug design. This means that treatments can be more precisely tailored to each individual patient's needs.

Clinical trials also benefit greatly from the integration of AI. AI algorithms are used to analyze vast amounts of data, including patient data and trial results, to determine the most effective treatments and to identify any potential safety concerns. This leads to a better understanding of the treatments and an improved patient experience.

Additionally, AI helps to speed up the clinical trial process by reducing the time it takes to enroll patients and complete trials. This results in faster approval of new treatments, which can be life-saving for patients in need.

In short, the integration of AI into the drug development and clinical trial process has been a game-changer. It has improved the efficiency and effectiveness of the process

and has led to better patient outcomes.

CHAPTER IV

AI in Education and Research

The impact of Artificial Intelligence (AI) on education and research has been remarkable. This cutting-edge technology has changed the way we approach learning and discovery, leading to more personalized and effective outcomes.

In education, AI is being leveraged to personalize the learning experience for students. AI algorithms assess a student's performance and learning style to create tailored lesson plans and assessments, resulting in improved student achievement.

In the realm of research, AI has revolutionized the way we analyze data and make new discoveries. AI algorithms can identify patterns in data sets that were previously undetectable, leading to faster and more accurate research. This can then be applied to real-world problems and lead to breakthroughs in fields like biology and astrophysics.

Moreover, AI is streamlining the research process by assisting researchers with data management and analysis. This saves time and reduces the risk of errors, resulting in more efficient and accurate research.

AI is transforming education and research in exciting ways. It's leading to more personalized and effective learning experiences for students, as well as faster and more accurate research. As AI continues to advance, we can expect to see even greater impacts in the future.

Advancements in natural language processing and machine translation

The advancements in natural language processing (NLP) and machine translation have been significant in recent years, due to the rapid development of Artificial Intelligence (AI) technology. NLP and machine translation are two of the most prominent areas in which AI is having a transformative impact on how we communicate and process information.

NLP is the technology that enables machines to understand, interpret, and generate human language. This has led to the development of virtual assistants, chatbots, and other language-based applications that have become an integral part of our daily lives. NLP is also being used to analyze vast amounts of text data to uncover trends, insights, and patterns that were previously difficult to detect.

Machine translation, on the other hand, is the technology that enables computers to translate text or speech from one language to another in real-time. This has made it possible to communicate and collaborate with people from around the world, breaking down language barriers and making the world a smaller place. Machine translation is also being used to translate vast amounts of text data, making it possible to analyze and understand information from other cultures and languages.

The advancements in NLP and machine translation have greatly impacted the way we communicate and process information. These technologies are helping to break down language barriers, making it easier for people to communicate and collaborate with others from around the world. As AI continues to advance, we can expect even more exciting developments in NLP and machine translation in the future.

Improving research and data analysis in various fields

The application of AI in research and data analysis has completely transformed the way many industries operate. With the ability to process vast amounts of information at lightning speed and pinpoint patterns and correlations that may have otherwise gone unnoticed, AI has taken the analysis game to a whole new level.

Take medicine for instance. AI algorithms are now being used to analyze patient data, predict outbreaks of diseases, and even provide personalized treatment plans. In finance, AI is being used to forecast stock prices, monitor market trends, and detect fraudulent activities. Marketing has also seen a boost from AI, as personalizing ads and marketing strategies with the help of algorithms leads to higher conversion rates and better customer engagement.

And the reach of AI in research continues to expand, as it is being utilized to examine scientific data, perform intricate simulations, and even discover new drugs and treatments. Environmental science has also greatly benefited from AI, with its help in analyzing satellite images and climate data to gain a deeper understanding of climate change and its impact.

All in all, AI has dramatically improved the way research and data analysis is done, making it faster and more precise. As AI continues to progress, we can look forward to even more advancements and breakthroughs in this field in the future.

AI-assisted education and online learning

AI has had a huge impact on the field of education, particularly with the rise of online learning. With AI-assisted education, students now have access to personalized learning experiences that cater to their unique strengths and weaknesses. AI algorithms can analyze student performance data to identify areas where they need more help, and provide customized lesson plans and exercises to fill in the gaps.

Additionally, AI has made online learning more accessible and effective. Chatbots and virtual assistants can provide immediate feedback to students and answer their questions, while machine learning algorithms can analyze student progress and make recommendations for further study. The use of AI in education has revolutionized the way students learn and has made education more accessible and effective for people of all ages and backgrounds.

CHAPTER V

AI in Society and Ethics

The rapid development and integration of AI into society has raised a number of ethical concerns, from privacy and data protection to the potential for AI to perpetuate existing biases and discrimination. The use of AI in decision-making processes, such as hiring, lending, and criminal justice, has also come under scrutiny for its potential to reinforce existing inequalities and perpetuate injustice.

Moreover, there is a growing concern about the potential for AI to take over jobs and disrupt the labor market, leading to job loss and economic inequality. The responsibility of AI developers and users to ensure that AI is used ethically and for the benefit of society has become a pressing issue.

In light of these concerns, it is important to have ongoing discussions and debates about the ethical use of AI. This includes developing ethical guidelines and best practices for the development and deployment of AI, as well as considering the role of government in regulating and overseeing the use of AI.

As AI continues to permeate our daily lives and impact every aspect of society, it is crucial that we proactively address the ethical implications of its use to ensure that AI benefits society as a whole.

The potential benefits and risks of AI

Artificial Intelligence (AI) holds tremendous potential for revolutionizing many aspects of our lives, from improving healthcare and education, to transforming industries such as finance, marketing, and manufacturing.

On the benefits side, AI has the potential to increase efficiency, accuracy, and speed in various fields. It can automate routine tasks and allow humans to focus on higher-level, creative, and problem-solving activities. AI can also provide real-time data analysis and decision-making support, enabling faster and more informed decision-making.

However, the development and deployment of AI also poses a number of risks. One of the main risks is job displacement, as AI systems and robots replace human workers in various industries. There is also a risk of AI perpetuating existing biases and discrimination, particularly in decision-making processes such as hiring, lending, and criminal justice.

Another risk is the potential for AI systems to be used maliciously, such as in cyber attacks or the spread of fake news and misinformation. There are also concerns about the privacy and security of data collected and processed by AI systems, as well as the potential for AI to reinforce existing inequalities and perpetuate injustice.

While AI holds immense potential for positive change, it is important to be aware of and address the potential risks associated with its development and deployment. This includes developing ethical guidelines and best practices for the development and use of AI, as well as considering the role of government in regulating and overseeing the use of AI.

Addressing the ethical concerns surrounding AI development and usage

As the capabilities of AI continue to grow and its applications become more widespread, there are growing concerns about the ethical implications of its development and usage. Some of the key ethical concerns surrounding AI include:

Bias and Discrimination: AI systems can perpetuate existing biases and discrimination, particularly in decision-making processes such as hiring, lending, and criminal justice. This can lead to unfair outcomes and perpetuate existing inequalities.

Job Displacement: AI has the potential to automate routine tasks and replace human workers, leading to job losses and economic disruption. This could have significant impacts on the job market and result in long-term economic and social problems.

Privacy and Security: AI systems collect and process large amounts of personal and sensitive data, raising concerns about privacy and security. There is also a risk of AI systems being used maliciously, such as in cyber attacks or the spread of fake news and misinformation.

Responsibility and Accountability: AI systems are becoming increasingly autonomous and capable of making decisions that have significant consequences. There is a need for clear lines of responsibility and accountability in the event of harm caused by AI systems.

To address these ethical concerns, it is important to develop ethical guidelines and best practices for the development and use of AI. This should include considering the impact of AI on human values and well-being, and ensuring that AI systems are designed and used in ways that respect human rights and dignity. It is also important to have ongoing public dialogue and debate about the ethical implications of AI, and to involve a wide range of stakeholders, including experts in AI, ethics, and law, as well as members of the public.

While AI has the potential to bring many benefits and improvements to our lives, it is important to carefully consider the ethical implications of its development and usage. By addressing these concerns, we can ensure that AI is developed and used in ways that benefit society as a whole, and that minimize any potential harm.

Discussing the role of governments and organizations in regulating AI

AI is a rapidly developing technology with the potential to revolutionize many aspects of our lives, but it also raises a number of ethical concerns. The use of AI can have far-reaching consequences, both positive and negative, and it is crucial that governments and organizations play a role in regulating its development and usage. This regulation must be grounded in a clear understanding of the potential benefits and risks of AI, as well as a commitment to addressing the ethical concerns surrounding its use. To be effective, these regulations must be comprehensive and well-informed, taking into account the unique challenges posed by AI and the various industries and sectors in which it is used. Ultimately, the goal must be to ensure that AI is used in ways that are safe, responsible, and in the best interests of all stakeholders.

CHAPTER VI

In conclusion, The future impact of 'AI' and it's needs, development

In conclusion, the impact of artificial intelligence on the world has been tremendous, and its influence will only continue to grow in the future. AI has the potential to revolutionize many industries, from healthcare and education to finance and marketing. In the realm of healthcare, AI has the potential to improve medical diagnoses and treatments, leading to more personalized care and better patient outcomes. In education and research, AI has the potential to assist in online learning, help with natural language processing and machine translation, and revolutionize data analysis in various fields.

However, along with the potential benefits, there are also important ethical and societal risks that must be addressed. The development and usage of AI must be guided by clear and responsible regulations, and organizations and governments must take a leading role in ensuring that AI is used in ways that benefit society as a whole. The future of AI is uncertain, but one thing is certain: it will shape the world in ways we can only imagine.

As we move forward, it is essential that we work together to ensure that AI is developed and used responsibly. We must strive to maximize its potential benefits while minimizing its risks, and make sure that it is accessible and inclusive for all. The future of AI is in our hands, and by working together, we can help to shape it in ways that make our world a better place for all. The impact of AI on the world has been immense, and its potential to shape the world in the future is limitless. The need for responsible AI development and usage has never been greater, and it is up to us to ensure that this new technology is used for the greater good.

Open Ai

OpenAI is a leading artificial intelligence research organization based in San Francisco, California. Founded in 2015, it has quickly established itself as one of the top organizations in the field of AI, with a mission to build safe and beneficial AI systems that can be used for the betterment of humanity. The organization is backed by some of the world's most prominent individuals and companies, including Elon Musk, Sam Altman, and Reid Hoffman, among others.

OpenAI conducts cutting-edge research in various areas of AI, including natural language processing, machine learning, robotics, and computer vision, among others. The organization's researchers are renowned experts in their respective fields and are dedicated to advancing the state of the art in AI. OpenAI's research findings are published in academic journals and conferences, making them widely accessible to the research community and the general public.

OpenAI's impact on the world of AI has been substantial. Its research has led to significant advances in various areas of AI and has helped to shape the direction of the field. For example, OpenAI's work in developing GPT-3, one of the largest and most powerful language models ever created, has opened up new possibilities for natural language processing and has sparked a wave of innovation in this area.

In addition to conducting research, OpenAI also engages in various outreach activities to educate and inform the public about the potential benefits and risks of AI. The organization is committed to promoting responsible AI development and usage and works closely with stakeholders from academia, industry, and government to promote best practices and ethical principles in AI.

Overall, OpenAI is an essential player in the world of AI and its impact will be felt for many years to come. Its dedication to advancing the field of AI and promoting responsible AI development and usage make it a key player in shaping the future of the technology and its impact on society.

9 798889 751922

Printed by Libri Plureos GmbH in Hamburg,
Germany